Snapshots *from the* Wedding

GARY SOTO

illustrated by

STEPHANIE GARCIA

PAPERSTAR

Penguin Young Readers Group

GLOSSARY

pobrecito   poor little guy

guapo   handsome, good looking

mira   Look! (look here)

mi abuela   my grandmother

mariachis   Mexican musical ensemble

pollo con mole   chicken with ground chile sauce

arroz y frijoles   rice and beans

tortilla   thin, round bread made from
cornmeal or wheat flour

guitarrón   Mexican bass guitar

de veras   honestly, truly

tío   uncle

tía   aunt

PaperStar
Published by Penguin Group
Penguin Young Readers Group, 345 Hudson Street, New York, New York 10014, U.S.A.
Penguin Books Ltd, 80 Strand, London WC2R 0RL, England
Penguin Books Australia Ltd, 250 Camberwell Road, Camberwell, Victoria 3124, Australia
Penguin Books Canada Ltd, 10 Alcorn Avenue, Toronto, Ontario, Canada M4V 3B2
Penguin Books (N.Z.) Ltd, 182-190 Wairau Road, Auckland 10, New Zealand

First published in 1997 by G. P. Putnam's Sons
This PaperStar edition published in 1998 by The Putnam & Grosset Group.

11 12 13 14 15 16 17 18 19 20

LIBRARY OF CONGRESS CATALOGING-IN-PUBLICATION DATA
Soto, Gary, Snapshots from the wedding / by Gary Soto; illustrated by Stephanie Garcia.   p.   cm.
Summary: Maya, the flower girl, describes a Mexican American wedding through snapshots of the day's events,
beginning with the procession to the altar and ending with her sleeping after the dance.
[1. Weddings—Fiction. 2. Mexican Americans—Fiction.] I. Garcia, Stephanie, ill. II. Title
PZ7.S7242Sn 1997 [E]—dc20 95-5793 CIP AC
ISBN 978-0-698-11752-5

Type design by Cecilia Yung and Donna Mark. The text is set in Stempel Schneidler Medium.

The three-dimensional artwork for this book was created with Sculpy clay, acrylic paints, wood, fabric, and a variety of found objects.

Manufactured in China

*Para
José-Luis Orozco
un compadre*
—G.S.

*To the unforgettable memories of
Aunt Esther
and her magical wedding day*
—S.G.

Here's me, Maya,
Flower girl with flowers in my hair.
I'm biting back a smile
Because I can see my silly cousin Isaac in the pews.
He's wiggling his tongue
In the space between his baby teeth,
White as Chiclets.

Here's a boy named Danny bearing a pillow with rings.
If he looked down, he would see that his left shoe is untied.
If he looked up, he would see his mother snapping his picture,
Little gentleman with combed hair.

There are bridesmaids, one taller than the next,
And the groomsmen, straight as soldiers.
There is Father Jaime,
And a yawning altar boy with a dirty tennis shoe peeking
From under his robe.

Here comes the beautiful bride, Isabel,
Her hands soft as doves.
Her steps are slow,
And the music is a slow march to the altar.
The candles sparkle, almost heart-shaped with flame
And almost as bright as her eyes.

There's Rafael,
A really, really nice guy,
But, *pobrecito*, a cast on his arm.
(Playing weekend softball, he slid into home,
Scored, but broke his wrist.)

I think it makes him look brave *y guapo*.

Mira, can you see Tía Marta crying big tears?
See Tío Juan itching in his new suit?

Isabel and Rafael say, "I do, I do,"
And they kiss longer than I want to look.

(You can't see it,
But I remember someone sneezing really loudly
And someone kicking the pew.)

And then there are lots of cameras flashing
And some mothers crying,
And one newborn baby crying,
Which starts two other babies crying,
Which starts Isabel crying,
She is so happy.

Here's rice coming down like rain.
Here's Danny crying because he got some in his eyes,

And look at me with my mouth open,
Catching the rice with my tongue.

This is the parking lot.
Tío Trino is always helping people, like in this one.
He is jump-starting somebody's car,
Careful not to smudge oil on his tuxedo.

If you look closely,
You can see the limousine driving away
And the trail of cars following.
Some flowers pasted on the hood are flying off.

At the reception
There's keg beer cooling in tubs,
And sodas on a table,
Potato chips and a bowl of olives.

Look at silly me. I push black olives
Onto my fingers
And wiggle them before I chomp them down.

Here's the wedding cake,
Seventh wonder of the world, from Blanco's Bakery,
With more frosting than a mountain of snow,
With more roses than *mi abuela*'s back yard,
With more swirls than a hundred turns on a merry-go-round.

Here, in this one, the mariachis have arrived.
The violinists look at Rafael's cast,
So scared for themselves.
After all, have you ever seen a violin player
With a broken arm?

First there is a toast to the bride and groom,
And then there are words—
Isabel, first graduate from college,
Rafael, first man to hit a home run
With his eyes closed. (I think it was a joke.)
Then everyone claps and some people hug the bride
A hundred times, it looks like to me.

Then we line up for *pollo con mole*,
Arroz y frijoles,
Then some soda or beer.

I splatter some *mole* on my dress.
I get some on my white anklet socks.
It is so good when you smear some on a *tortilla*.

Then the mariachis begin,
Trumpet blaring, the *guitarrón* thumping a beat,
The violins squeaking like mice,
The guitar singing like a bird cupped in your hands.

The new couple dance,
And then parents, then maybe grandparents,
Then the bride dances for money.
Tío Julio pins a twenty on her dress,
Then I see my daddy press a check into the bride's palm.

While the grown-ups dance,
We skid down the hallway,
Shoes off. Then we play hide-and-seek,
And then spit water at each other

And whack each other with balloons,
And then race up the stairway,
Where at the top a red sign glows EX T.

Then the dancing really starts, the mariachis grow red-faced,
And—*de veras*—I think I see a fat tongue
Stick out from the end of the trumpet,
And a mouse drop from the violin,
And a bird fly from the guitar.
Or maybe I'm getting sleepy.

But I wake up when the cake is cut,
A slice shared by the new couple.
I line up with my plate,
And when I get my piece, I get a rose
And a little ribbon of green.

Then Isabel throws her bouquet,
And it's caught by the tallest woman there,
My cousin Virginia, a college basketball player,
With a three-foot vertical leap.

Then the mariachis leave,
And a band called Los Teardrops arrives.
Everyone dances to the oldies but goodies,
Even me, as I ride on my daddy's shoes.

And this is me, asleep in the car.
If you look closely you can see some *mole*
On my chin, a little taste I woke up to
The next morning.

It was a wedding to remember.